The Shadows that Rush Past

A Collection of Frightening Inuit Folktales

INHABIT
MEDIA

Inhabit Media Inc.

Iqaluit • Toronto

Published by Inhabit Media Inc.
www.inhabitmedia.com

Inhabit Media Inc. (Iqaluit) P.O. Box 11125, Iqaluit, Nunavut, X0A 1H0
(Toronto) 191 Eglinton Avenue East, Suite 310, Toronto, Ontario, M4P 1K1

Edited by: Louise Flaherty and Neil Christopher
Written by: Rachel Qitsualik-Tinsley
Art Direction by: Neil Christopher
Illustrations by: Emily Fiegenschuh and Larry MacDougall
Cover Artwork by: Emily Fiegenschuh

We acknowledge the support of the Canada Council for the Arts for our publishing program.

This project was made possible in part by the Government of Canada

ISBN 978-1-77227-218-5

Printed in Canada

Library and Archives Canada Cataloguing in Publication

Qitsualik-Tinsley, Rachel, 1953–, author
The shadows that rush past : a collection of frightening Inuit folktales / written by Rachel A. Qitsualik ; illustrated by Emily Fiegenschuh, Larry MacDougall.

ISBN 978-1-77227-218-5 (softcover)

1. Inuit--Folklore. 2. Inuit mythology--Juvenile literature.
I. Fiegenschuh, Emily, illustrator II. MacDougall, Larry, illustrator
III. Title.

E99.E7Q28 2018   j398.2089'9712   C2018-904178-1

 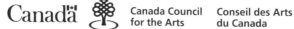

Canada   Canada Council   Conseil des Arts
          for the Arts   du Canada

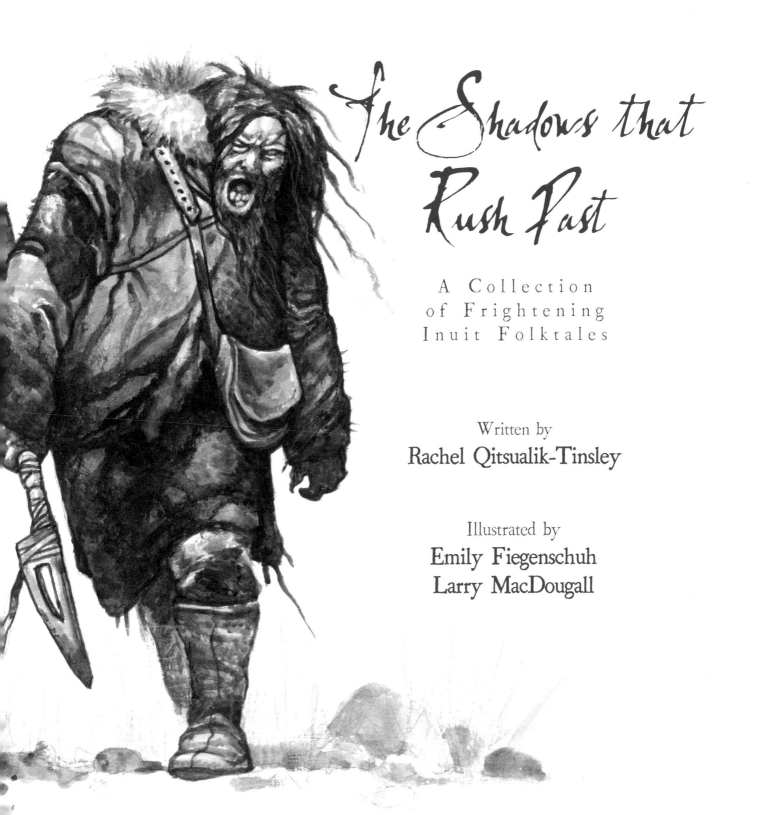

The Shadows that Rush Past

A Collection of Frightening Inuit Folktales

Written by
Rachel Qitsualik-Tinsley

Illustrated by
Emily Fiegenschuh
Larry MacDougall

Contents

INTRODUCTION

The ancestors of Inuit were imaginative people. That imagination, born of ice, glacial stone, and a Land that is impossible to fully comprehend, shows in their arts. Look at a carving, inspired by spiritual themes. Look at a print. It is as though the ancestors of Inuit, the *Sivulivinit*, have become dreams that lend power to living minds.

Of all imaginative expressions, however, the story is the form most treasured by Inuit. Such tales are codes. Dream-histories. Sacred works and delights. In past efforts to destroy our culture, the traditional stories were heavily attacked, since they were recognized for what they are—tools that empower the minds of Inuit, linking them to their ancestry.

Think about that for a heartbeat or two.

All of these tales are fun, brimming with unique monsters, clever escapes, and strange forces that thrive in the Land. But they are also glimpses into the minds of generations long past. Some of the stories are thousands of years old, recognizable all around the wide Arctic! It is amazing to think that an elder, ten or more centuries ago, would have felt a personal connection to these tales. But it is true. In that sense, the stories are more than mere time machines. Defying death and decay, they are the songs of immortality. They allow us to understand the passions, the wants and needs, the imaginations of generations who could never have imagined our own age. They are the greatest of gifts, surviving because of an oral tradition that is as crafty and enduring as Inuit themselves. And, like hardy blossoms that close against the chill, only to open again when the sun next warms them, these tales are ready for written form.

Fear these stories. Laugh. Relax, and allow

yourself to feel what the ancient Inuit felt. Believe what they believed, because their world was no less real than ours. Through your sense of wonder, your own wisdom, and your understanding of what these tales really say, the ancient imagination remains immortal.

Pijariiqpunga (all I have to say).

AMAUTALIK

There came a late winter when a little boy went out to play in the snow. Nobody is sure of the boy's name, though he must have been a tough little thing, since fate would demand a lot from him.

You see, it also happened that he had chosen a bad time to play. The Land is bursting with beauty, but it also has its share of horrors to offer. One such horror is the *amautalik*. Imagine an old woman. Then, in your mind's eye, make her gigantic, maybe twice the size of a large grown-up. Make her filthy, too, with leathery skin and big, greedy, fishlike eyes. Later, I'll tell you what is under her parka, though I don't think you'll like it. What matters, for now, is her back. She seems to be hunched, but don't be fooled. She actually has a kind of storage place on her shoulders, and that is where she keeps the people she has kidnapped. That's right; she's a thief of people. Especially children.

Back to our boy. The poor kid didn't get to play for long before the hulking figure of the amautalik came leaping after him. He had time enough to scream as fingers, their nails dirtied with old skin from the amautalik scratching herself, reached out and seized him. The boy might as well have been grabbed by stone. There was no chance to struggle. With a speed born of practice, the monster stuffed the child into the place on her back (some say it's a hood; others imagine it as a cage; personally, I don't want

to think about it). The amautalik managed to lope away just as the boy's family arrived, wondering why the child had cried out.

The family stood stunned, watching the amautalik's huge form wind among ridges and low mounds of ice, gradually disappearing from sight. Before the monster managed to get away, though, the boy's grandmother (the only one who really understood what was happening) called upon special powers. She was an *angakkuq* (shaman), you see, so she didn't have to stand helplessly while her grandson was being stolen. In a single heartbeat, she hurled her *ulu* (crescent knife) and a curse after the amautalik. The ulu carried her curse, fluttering like a butterfly as it chased the amautalik across the Land. When it caught up with the monster, the blade struck. It did not hurt the amautalik physically, but instead imparted the grandmother's Strength. This was a special kind of Strength, not having anything to do with muscle, running as much through the Land as through people. Like the beginnings of a disease, the curse began to eat at the monster's mind.

Eventually, the amautalik came to her *igluvigaq* (snow house) and plucked the child from her back. For the boy, it was the start of a time of slavery, in a terrible, terrible place. Some say that, among the horrors in that igluvigaq, there were living heads—past victims of the monster— that whispered to or babbled at the child. But the amautalik did not collect the boy's head. Instead, she used him as a servant.

I warned you that I would tell you what was under her parka. Wriggling among the flaking folds of her skin were lice. The size of puppies. Wherever they bit the amautalik, they drank blood, and the monster never stopped scratching at the wounds. The boy's job, then, was to help her remove such creatures. It was an unending task. Days went by, but the lice were in endless supply. The boy wept continually as the lice bit him and sampled his blood. The amautalik's mind continued to decay, buckling under the grandmother's curse. Still, the monster clung to her slave. In her confusion, she even came to call him "son."

In the meantime, the real family of the boy was still looking for him. Even the grandmother participated, sending out her helper—a snow bunting—to search every part of the Land. Don't think of a regular bird. This was a special bunting, fairly smart, and chatty. The bunting's hard work paid off, and he eventually spotted the amautalik's igluvigaq. Just as soon as the bird had notified his mistress (the boy's grandmother) he was sent out once more, ahead of a rescue party consisting of the boy's parents and other relatives.

The bunting, being a sharp little guy, didn't reveal himself right away. Perching near the door of the amautalik's igluvigaq, he waited until the monster was asleep. As it happened, the boy had just finished picking lice off the amautalik, so that while she slept in comfort, the child sat quietly weeping, covered in louse bites.

Cautiously, the bird drew the boy's attention. But there was no time for comforting words, and the bunting-helper urged the boy not to risk running out of the igluvigaq to find his parents, lest the monster awaken. Instead, the helper explained that when the time was right, he would complete the grandmother's Strong curse, allowing the boy to slip away unnoticed.

The amautalik awakened, demanding to know why her "son" was regarding

something outside of the igluvigaq. But the boy drew inspiration from the bravery and wit of the little bird. He managed to deceive the amautalik with gentle words, making her think that he had been curious about some ravens that had settled nearby. Tired, and more confused than ever, the monster returned to sleep.

When the amautalik next awakened, it was to a bunting's chirps. She sat up, blinking, to see that a little bird flew round and round the inward sloping walls of the igluvigaq. Her great, watery eyes could barely track the bunting, as it was so fast. As the monster watched the helper, and the voice of the bunting taunted her, the amautalik's mind became wholly entangled in the grandmother's curse. Stupid, unthinking, with her eyes and ears bound by the little bird's antics, the amautalik sat like something frozen in ice.

At first creeping, then dashing, the boy could wait no longer. He fled the igluvigaq of horror, leaving his grandmother's helper to finish dealing with the amautalik. He staggered. He stumbled. And, nearly blind with panic, he ran into the outstretched arms of his parents.

There were many more tears. These, however, were of the good sort. I told you, the Land also has its beauty.

Pijariiqpunga (all I have to say).

AKHLA

Imagine the oldest person you've ever met. This story is older than the grandparents of the grandparents of that person's grandparents. Maybe that's why no one can now agree on the sort of monster at the heart of the tale. Some people call it the *akla*, while others call it *aklak* or *akhla*, to mention a few. Today, all such words mean "brown bear," but you only have to hear a little of this story to realize that it's no tale of a simple animal.

This creature—whatever it was, let's call it akhla—was something like a cross between a grizzly bear and a human being. It was large, and it certainly used tools. It also ate people, and not simply because it was starving or trying them out for flavour. Some say that, back in the days when nature was not yet fully formed, when the Land was crawling with weird things, there was an akhla who raided graves on the edge of a particular camp. You can imagine how hard that was for those camp folk. Inuit used to pile many stones over their dead. Yet the akhla was strong enough to remove all such stones, and its appetite became a problem.

There was a man, however, who offered to help the camp folk. In the far west, some called him Upaum. In the east, he was known as Kiviuq. Others simply called him the Man. He was a great hunter, a far traveller; but mostly, he was a powerful *angakkuq* (shaman), and had little fear of a lone akhla.

The Man thought long and hard on how to catch the akhla—no easy feat, since, while the monster was a bit stupid, it was neither weak nor unwary. The Man at last realized that he would not be able to catch the akhla; though, if he called upon his powers in a risky way, he might at least find the monster by allowing himself to be caught.

If you could have seen into the Man's head, knowing his thoughts, you probably would have warned him not to take such a gamble. Yet no one stopped him as he set out alone, upon the chilly Land, and there worked his powers.

The Man fell to the ground, as though frozen and dead. Some say that he allowed himself to be buried under stones, as one who has been laid to rest—or even, according to a few, like frozen meat that's been cached for the winter. All Inuit agree, however, that the akhla eventually found him. And, since the monster was not a picky eater and had no reason to suspect that it had happened upon an angakkuq imitating a frozen corpse, the creature took this free food back to its home.

By the time the akhla arrived at its *iglu* (snow house), the monster was exhausted. The akhla was a huge, towering creature, able to stride across the wide Land and its hills, travelling far before it tired; but the Man had used up all its strength. As the Man, pretending to be a frozen body, had been carried upside-down the whole time, he had grasped at willow stems and rocks whenever the akhla's eyes had been turned away. Now, the akhla was too tired to think straight, and it flung the Man on a bench inside the iglu, wanting to rest while its latest meal thawed.

There was no way that one might have distinguished the Man from a corpse, still and lifeless on that bench, though the Man's mind was quite active. He was worried now, even a bit frightened, since he'd heard the noises of a whole inhuman family while being carried into the camp. He realized that there was more than one akhla in this place. What to do? If he sprang to "life," he might find himself overwhelmed by the clan of monsters. So he decided to remain as he was, thinking through his situation, all the while lying with eyes pressed shut. Panic, and the urge to leap up and run like a hare, bit into him; yet only by lying still as death, he sensed, might he escape death itself.

As it happened, the Man came to feel as though strange objects—two things, actually, both warm and wet—were brushing at his face. Startled, horrified, he could no longer keep his eyes closed, and his lids cracked open so that he saw twin faces, the mingled features of beast and human, looming over his own. They were, he realized, the akhla's children. Impatient to eat, they had begun to lick the Man.

The akhla-children were startled by the sight of the Man, their dinner, looking back at them.

"Father!" they cried. "The meat just opened its eyes!"

"Whatever," said the akhla, perhaps not taking the children seriously. "I dragged it far enough. Let it do whatever it does."

While the inhuman children argued with their father, the Man shuddered with panic, understanding that he had to take quick action. His eyes, now fully open, spotted an axe near the doorway. He rolled off the bench and seized the tool. The akhla was still resting, eyes closed, while the monstrous children pleaded for him to rise. But it was too late. The Man struck, killing the akhla with a blow.

With the monster-children still shrieking at his back, the Man fled the iglu, axe in hand. His plan had not quite unfolded the way he'd had in mind. Staggering, he got his bearings, then dashed past the akhla-mother, who was bent over a fire outside the iglu, overly preoccupied with tending to a bag of human fat that she had prepared. The akhla-mother was so busy that she'd ignored the wails of her children, and noticed the Man only as his axe swung at her. Perhaps the Man had intended the blow to sink into her skull, as it already had with her husband's, but the Man was running at full tilt. Slashing in a wild arc, the blade instead met the bag of fat, rupturing it.

The akhla-mother snarled at the Man, roaring as might a great bear, and stood,

torn as to whether she should pursue him or stem the flow of wasted fat. After a moment, she let the Man go, fixing her precious bag as best she could. She knew that she was much faster than a human man and that she'd easily catch him, even after taking the time to fix her ruined bag.

The Man glanced backward no more than once, letting his legs carry him with great speed over low hills, around boulders, across narrow valleys. The entire while, his mind raced faster than his feet, thinking: *What to do? What to do?* The first akhla, the father, had been no genius, and it was a good bet that the mother was no more clever than he. Yet cleverness no longer mattered, did it? The akhla-mother was no human being. She was undoubtedly faster than the Man. She was tougher. She was stronger. And, from the moment she caught him, she would rip until his insides were his outside.

A roar, not far distant, confirmed that the akhla-mother had caught the Man's scent. Over one hill or another, she would soon arrive. If he could not think of a way to apply his powers before she caught him . . .

Like a flash of moonlight through thick cloud, an idea came to the Man. He had no time to think it out, but only stopped on the open Land, lungs heaving. After forcing calm upon his mind, he stooped, holding his middle finger downward. In that position, he stared at the Land below his feet until he felt as though the Land were staring back at him. He squatted long enough to draw a line with his middle finger, a sort of brushstroke across level ground. Then he felt the Land's call, like a sudden tug, to which he responded—and power flowed between himself and the earth. These were the days, you see, when human beings recognized the Land as one might a dear relative; and the Land, in turn, recognized humankind.

The Man then leapt over the invisible line he'd drawn, chanting the power-words,

"Where is the river?"

By the time the Man's feet landed on the other side, he could hear a trickling noise behind him. He ran—chanting, laughing, still drawing on the might of the Land—until he stood at a safe distance from the river that he knew was forming behind him. The more power that flowed between himself and the Land, the more water appeared. And when the Man at last turned, standing drained after his great effort, he saw that his power had taken on a will of its own. He had intended to create a small river as a barrier between himself and the akhla-mother. But this was no simple river. Here, before his gaze, raged a torrent.

The Man stood exhausted for some time, having little strength to do anything but stare, as the akhla-mother at last crested a low hill. She spotted him instantly, making her way to the river's edge.

From opposite sides, the two enemies stood glaring at one another.

In time, the she-akhla began to watch the water's flow, as though she were studying it. Up and down the riverbank, she paced.

"How did you cross this?" she eventually asked, calling across the noise of the water.

The Man, by now, had collected his wits. He took his time in answering, phrasing his reply with great care.

"I drank it up," he called back.

The she-akhla nodded, though she didn't at first answer. Today, people dispute the reply she made, or whether she answered the Man at all. Whatever the case, she was proud and mighty. If she answered, she might have said,

"I, too, am an angakkuq. If you can manage this, human, so can I. Watch me drink the river as you did, and know that nothing can keep you safe from me."

The Man waited, hoping that she would do as she'd claimed. He saw her wade into the waters, watched her stoop to drink the river down. He could feel the Strength of

her as she tried to do so, her angakkuq power playing itself out upon the currents—and, for a moment, he grew afraid, wondering if she truly might have the power to consume what he'd created.

Yet the river flowed on.

Still, the she-akhla drank, her face concealed by the waters rushing over it, and out poured her own power.

Untold time passed, the Man waiting, anxious, the she-akhla drinking, until she began to swell. As she swelled, the edges of her body grew hazy, and the colour bled from her. She became transparent, as if she were taking on something of the water's nature, rather than bringing it under her own control.

And the Man sighed with relief, knowing that he'd won.

The Man watched, patient, and time saw the she-akhla's form come apart, becoming ghostly, stretching out across the water as a great, floating fog. And the Man stood amazed, since this was an early period of the world when no one had ever before witnessed such a now-common thing as mist.

Here, then, is an origin—one small part of the world, born out of a story that Inuit knew when they were one folk. Today, depending on which people are asked, the river still flows, and some may claim that it's a river near their own community. Again, as with whether one says akla or aklak or akhla, it's a simple detail.

All Inuit, however, agree that it was one Man who tricked the she-akhla into drinking the river. All agree that she failed. She, like her husband, no longer lives, though she's remembered in the existence of fog.

Pijariiqpunga (all I have to say).

Nanurluk

It was far to the north that the hunter, Nakasungnak, was said to have met his strange fate. There, after all of Nakasungnak's wandering, he settled among a terrified people. They had good reason to be afraid. They were the victims of a great bear that appeared from time to time. Huge. Murderous. It killed at will, and drove the people in all directions, when they were not in hiding.

Was the monster really anything special, though? Nakasungnak wondered. He wasn't a useless hunter, and, like most Inuit his age, he'd dealt with bears before.

All who talked to Nakasungnak of the bear, especially when the hunter went on about how he might deal with the beast, cried, "No!" Was Nakasungnak actually stupid enough to believe that an entire camp of people would fear one ordinary bear? Well, perhaps. Nakasungnak, like some people, was difficult to talk to. It wasn't that he was dense, exactly. He simply liked to listen to the ideas in his head more than the words of others. So he didn't pay much attention to the camp people when they explained just how large this bear was.

It wasn't long before Nakasungnak saw the bear with his own eyes, however, and realized that the people of the camp had not exaggerated. There was no warning—not the usual yips and howls of the camp dogs—as the bear approached. The creature was monstrous, larger than the hills closest to the camp, and it stamped in upon the shore of

the place like a man crushing ice under heel. The camp people were terrified as ever, but Inuit will fight fiercely when it counts, and the massive bear's side soon prickled with harpoons and arrows cast or shot by the men, which gave the women time enough to usher children to safety. But if such weapons affected the bear, would it have continued to attack time and again? No, the bear raked and bit at all within sight, crushing even nearby rocks under its vast bulk. It noticed harpoons no more than it might the nip of newborn pups.

When Nakasungnak saw the bear, he was startled, eyes wide, standing rigid as stone. Because he had listened to his own thoughts over those of the camp elders, he'd failed to absorb the fact that this was no ordinary bear. It was one of those monsters some call the *nanurluk*, which others call the "ice-covered bear," and all refer to with fear. It was awesome, looming, hungry, and ancient. How might even the best of men, much less Nakasungnak with his silly knife in hand, rise to this creature's level?

It is the way of life, however, that even the oddest personality quirk can turn out to be a gift in the right situation. And as Nakasungnak stood, watching the bear make a ruin out of the camp that had shown him kindness, the blood of his ancestors boiled within him. With a dreadful scream, he ran down toward the shore, where the bear rampaged. All the way, his knife was held out before him, as though he'd become a human arrow, with his little blade as the tip, though he gave no thought to how it might impress itself on such a bear. Fired by his own strange thoughts—the idea that he would somehow kill this nanurluk, no matter what—he simply charged.

Having just killed several camp people and scattered the rest, the bear's attention was caught by this scream of Nakasungnak's—not the usual sound of fear, but a wail of crazy anger. But the monster was hardly afraid of one more tiny person, so it lowered its head, bellowing its own fury back at the approaching Nakasungnak. For a moment, the two enemies remained that way: bear looming like some ivory hill, man running with outstretched knife, both roaring.

Then Nakasungnak ran straight into the nanurluk's mouth.

The bear reared, startled, and Nakasungnak slipped on the creature's great black tongue, saliva covering his boots like hot slush. But momentum was with him, and Nakasungnak fell forward, into the bear's throat. It was probably a good thing, since the bear's response to having a person in its mouth was to snap its jaws closed, and if Nakasungnak's legs had still been dangling outside the mouth when that had happened, well, a pair of boots might have fallen to the beach, feet still in them. As it was, darkness engulfed Nakasungnak. Head first, he became lodged in the bear's gullet. The bear's response was to gag. Nakasungnak could feel the great walls of that slimy tunnel hugging his sides, and his rage cleared, leaving panic. There were only two directions to go, he realized in a flash: backward into the bear's mouth or forward into the darkness of its stomach. For a moment, there was some hope that the bear would cough him out, but then the monster's throat began to convulse.

And down went Nakasungnak.

The camp folk, standing among the ruin of their tents, screamed as they watched the bear swallow Nakasungnak. They prepared to run, knowing that they were next to be devoured.

Then, an even stranger thing happened.

The bear stood utterly still for a long moment, its muzzle lowered. The great head swayed from side to side. A shudder ran through the beast, making harpoons and arrows quiver across its vast, ivory pelt. The bear opened its mouth, tongue rolling, and it became obvious that the bear was trying to vomit. Then the monster seemed to panic, racing up and down the beach, thundering, further smashing already floating bits of boat (and a body or two) under paws wider than tent rings. The black claws dug furrows across the beach, casting rock and soil in all directions. And onlookers screamed as the bear turned, running up into what little remained of the camp.

Instead of continuing in its attack, however, the bear stopped—though most people kept running. The few who remained to study the bear saw it sway once more, then shudder again and again. When the shuddering stopped, the bear's legs collapsed. As people watched, their jaws dangling in awe, the bear rolled over onto its side, and lay still as stone.

It took the people some time to verify that the nanurluk was dead. After all, experienced hunters will not trust even an ordinary bear that, at first, seems dead. How many inexperienced men have been mauled when such bears leap up again? After some time, the remaining camp folk felt that it was safe enough to approach the nanurluk's carcass, a body that lay like some ice-encrusted hill where their tents had once been.

The people were just beginning to calm themselves when further strangeness presented itself. Along one great wall of the bear's side, the yellowed fur of its pelt seemed to blossom with red. The crimson colour, that of blood, spread, and those who saw it cried out, calling the other camp folk to come witness the event. Within a moment, the entire camp stood watching. Many arrived just in time to note that a gore-darkened knife was working its way back and forth through the bear's heavy flesh—from the inside out.

It took less than a minute, after that, for Nakasungnak's arm, then head, to emerge. The young hunter cried out, gasping for air, as he wormed his way free of the path he'd carved in the bear's side. At last, some of the camp people shook themselves free of shock, and stepped forward to help Nakasungnak out of the gaping wound.

It took some time to clean the shivering Nakasungnak off, and while he was tended to, he explained how he'd been left with little choice once swallowed down into the suffocating darkness of the bear's gut. With blade still in hand, Nakasungnak had only cut and cut and cut. Unthinking, he had wielded his knife in whatever direction availed itself, praying for escape.

The camp folk were overjoyed that Nakasungnak, despite all warnings of the elders, had beaten the odds and become the greatest bear-slayer in memory. He was their hero, and they were sensitive enough to keep from him the fact that the bear's digestive acid had left him with less hair than a newborn baby. When Nakasungnak realized this fact, however, his vanity got the best of him and he ran off to his tent in embarrassment.

It has never been told whether or not, once poor Nakasungnak recovered, he enjoyed his status as a hero—though we can probably assume that he did. Maybe he enjoyed it a bit too much. The nanurluk's vast carcass, as food alone, lasted long into the winter months, so that Nakasungnak's reputation as a hunter was fixed for all time. But the one thing that seems to have remained hungry within him was Nakasungnak's own ambition—for that is the way of ego, which is why the elders have always cautioned against it.

That land, unnamed and far, far to the north, was full of odd beings, and Nakasungnak seems to have made a special point of showing fearlessness before all such creatures. Perhaps, as usual, it was simply that he couldn't hear the voices of others over the ideas babbling in his own head. The local elders and hunters often tried to advise Nakasungnak on how to approach the strange animals of that area—birds that could speak like people, or fish whose eyes were set on one side of their head—but Nakasungnak, full of confidence because of how he'd dealt with the nanurluk, ignored every word of warning. He always craved a sight of the land's bizarre offerings, and therefore saw nothing.

There arrived a day, it is told, when the camp people got ready for clouds of biting, stinging insects. They prepared, as they did in every such season, to enclose themselves in their tents in order to avoid the bugs. But not Nakasungnak. At last, he thought, another day had come when he could distinguish himself; when he could show the people that he alone might stand against that which the best of them feared. After all, the encounter with the ice-covered bear had worked out, hadn't it?

The elders, the hunters, the women, even the children urged Nakasungnak to take shelter in a tent and seal it tight. These were not normal insects, they told him, but monsters bigger than a man's fist—large as seabirds. They were hungry for meat, and if just one of them stung Nakasungnak, it would be as if he'd been shot with an arrow. But these cautions only made Nakasungnak more determined than ever to witness the insects with his own eyes. Killer bugs that no one had ever withstood? He liked the odds. This was, according to the way his mind worked, a return to that day with the monstrous nanurluk. As usual, how might any word of wisdom be heard over the noise of Nakasungnak's own head?

In time, the sky darkened, and every one of the camp folk disappeared into tents—all but Nakasungnak. He stood out in the open for a time, the final, pleading calls of the camp people ringing in his ears. He wondered when he would see the strange bugs.

By the time he realized that the sky had not darkened from clouds, but from insects, it was too late.

After their period of shelter had gone by, and the camp people no longer heard the terrible noise of the stinging insects outside their tents, they emerged. Many called for Nakasungnak, but there was no answer. At last, down by the shore, someone noticed an overturned boat, guessing that Nakasungnak had tried, at the last moment, to crawl beneath it.

They uncovered only a skeleton.

Pijariiqpunga (all I have to say).

MAHAHA

There once was a married couple who lived alone. They were young. They loved one another dearly. But they lived in a time when all Inuit needed to hunt in order to eat, and all young men were hunters. So the husband set out to find food for himself and his wife, leaving the young wife alone in their *iglu* (snow house). The wife was not too upset to be left alone during the days when her husband was away, since she was busy. It was a time when Inuit had to make their own things in order to survive, so she had much work to do.

The wife was singing softly to herself when she heard a noise near the entrance to the iglu. She put her sewing down. She called out to her husband.

There was no reply. Still thinking that her husband might have returned, but maybe hadn't heard her call, she crawled into the iglu's narrow entrance tunnel, a sort of porch leading to the outside. Her eyes were on the hard-packed snow over which she crawled. For a moment, she saw only her breath. Snow. Her own hands.

Then she saw other hands—lean and grey, like dry, bloodless meat—grasping at her wrists. Screaming, she was pulled into middle of the porch. A humanlike creature scrambled over her, discoloured, almost naked, giggling. It pinned her down. And it was cold. Very cold. She gasped at the icy touch of its fingers as it reached under her top. Then it tickled

her. It was not a friendly tickle. It was not the tickle one might experience under a playful parent, or an aunt, or a sibling. The tickling was vicious. It was like being raked with icicles.

The young wife wept. She wanted to scream. She wanted to beg the manlike creature to stop. But the tickling stole her breath away. And the creature gave no hint of stopping, but only tickled harder, then harder, giggles rising into laughter as horrible as the tickling itself.

The torture went on, and the young wife ran out of breath.

The husband eventually returned from his hunt, and wept for a time over the lifeless body of his wife. Her flesh was frozen. Her eyes were open. Her mouth was open. The expression on her face, that of supreme horror and agony, tore at the husband's heart.

Hours passed, and the young hunter's grief turned into a new emotion. Rage. His eyes narrowed. He scanned the wintery landscape. He was wise enough to understand that no animal had killed his wife. And the marks on her body, the barefoot tracks in snow, reminded him of a creature spoken of by elders. It liked to tickle. It liked to laugh. It liked to kill. For this reason, the sound of its laughing, Inuit called it the *mahaha*. Had this thing murdered his wife? No one knew what a mahaha was. It was simply a creature of darkness and cold. It was manlike, but mad. Evil. The young husband wondered if the mahaha had really left. The creature was nowhere in sight, but that did not mean that it was not watching him, even now. Waiting for his back to be turned. Waiting for him to fall asleep.

So be it, thought the hunter. He would find out, for certain, if a mahaha had killed his wife by offering the creature something of interest.

Himself.

With tenderness, the young man disposed of his wife's body, then entered the iglu. He crawled into bed, covering himself as though to sleep. He did not sleep.

Hours passed. Wind howled. And there came a noise from the entrance to the iglu. The young hunter made sure to lie still, pretending to slumber. He listened, and heard something crawl into the iglu.

Nearer and nearer there came a shuffling sound. Soon, it was at the husband's bedside, and he felt someone paw at the caribou hides covering him. From less than a hand-span away, it seemed, there came a terrible voice.

"Father-in-law . . . ," it croaked, perhaps to mock him.

Then it giggled.

From under his blankets, the husband wondered if that giggle was the last thing his beautiful wife had heard, and his teeth bared in rage like those of a wolf. The young man rolled from his bed, lunged toward the mahaha, and his strong hunter's hands caught the icy ankles of the creature.

Bellowing in fury, the hunter stood, pulling the mahaha from its feet, so that the creature's head cracked against the hard floor of the iglu. Using all of his power, the hunter repeated this movement. As though he were cracking a whip rather than a manlike figure, the hunter flung the mahaha again and again, in blows that might have killed a human being half a dozen times over.

But the mahaha was not human.

With every strike, the mahaha laughed. Its laughter rose higher, higher, no matter how hard the young hunter lashed it. By the time the hunter ran out of breath, releasing the mahaha's ankles, the creature's laughter was at a fever pitch. The young husband fled the iglu before the mahaha could regain its footing. Now prey rather than hunter, his eyes were round with horror. The creature was too terrible. Too unnatural. He no longer wanted revenge. He wanted to get away. He wanted to be anywhere but near the mahaha.

And so he ran.

Wherever the young man ran, however, no matter how long, the mahaha followed. Hours passed. Sometimes, the husband looked over his shoulder, hoping to see nothing but ice and snow. But the mahaha was there. Loping. Laughing. Chasing him down like a wolf.

"Father-in-law!" it always cried. "Father-in-law!" Then the young man could run no more. His lungs burned like lamp flames in his chest. A last burst of energy brought him, in a great leap, over a crack in the ice. He was finished. He hunched, panting, while the mahaha approached the opposite side of the ice crack. Only water separated them now. The mahaha's calm breath could be seen on the chilly air. The

creature did not seem at all tired. It narrowed its eyes, huge and cruel, at the young husband. Its grey lips spread even further. Its grin showed far more teeth than any human mouth could hold.

"Wait," gasped the young man. "You've won. Just let me have a drink."
As though curious, the mahaha stood motionless, watching the young man kneel by the ice crack. The husband's trembling hand stretched out to scoop up some water. In strange imitation, maybe even mockery, the mahaha then copied the young man, doing exactly the same thing.

Instead of drinking, however, the young hunter's hand shot out to grab the mahaha by its wrist. Bellowing as he had back in the iglu, the hunter pulled the mahaha over the edge and into the ice crack. The mahaha fought, using all of its monstrous power, trying to catch the ice shelf's edge and pull itself out. Despite the freezing water, the young hunter always pushed the creature back in, holding its head below the surface. Within moments, the young man's arms were soaked and numb, but the memory of his beloved wife gave him strength.

In time, the mahaha no longer struggled. The hunter stood gasping, weeping, watching the creature's body disappear into the water's depths. In this way, the young hunter avenged his wife. In this way, he killed the mahaha.

Pijariiqpunga (all I have to say).

CONTRIBUTORS

RACHEL QITSUALIK-TINSLEY is a writer, folklorist, archaic language expert and elder, producing speculative fiction and educational works that showcase the secretive world of Arctic cosmology and shamanism. Of Inuit-Cree ancestry, Rachel was born in a tent at the northernmost tip of Baffin Island. Raised as a boy, she learned Inuit survival lore from her father—eventually surviving residential school. Rachel has witnessed the full transition of Inuit from traditional culture to information age, balancing personal shamanic experience with a university education. Rachel has published over 400 articles on culture and language, ranging over periodicals such as *Native Journal*, *Nunatsiaq News*, *News/North*, and the website Indian Country Today. In 2014, her first book on Inuit lore, *The Shadows that Rush Past*, was shortlisted for the Silver Birch Award and the Rocky Mountain Book Award. She has enjoyed several years as a judge for Historica's Indigenous Arts & Stories competition. In 2012, she was awarded a Queen Elizabeth II Diamond Jubilee Medal for contributions to Canadian culture. Together with her husband, Sean Qitsualik-Tinsley, she has published 10 books and many shorter works, most drawing from history or the fantastical thought and beliefs of Arctic traditions (e.g., Inuit and the now-extinct Tuniit). In 2014, their young adult novel of historical fiction, *Skraelings: Clashes in the Old Arctic*, won second prize in the Governor General's Literary Awards. The same novel won first prize in the Burt Award of 2015. For inspiration, Rachel draws from a deep love of nature and the "imaginal intelligence" of ancient cultures. Her works are included in course content at universities across Canada and abroad.

EMILY FIEGENSCHUH attended art school at the Ringling College of Art and Design in Sarasota, FL, and graduated with honors and a BFA from the Illustration program. She has illustrated numerous Dungeons and Dragons rulebooks for Wizards of the Coast and has contributed cover and interior illustrations to the novel series Knights of the Silver Dragon. She illustrated the ten-part fantasy story "The Star Shard" by Frederic S. Durbin for *Cricket Magazine*. Her art has also appeared in the *New York Times* bestsellers *A Practical Guide to Dragons* and *A Practical Guide to Monsters*. Emily lives with her husband in the Seattle area.

LARRY MACDOUGALL is an award-winning illustrator living in Stoney Creek, Ontario. Some of his recent projects include *The Secret History of Giants*, *Eragon's Guide to Alagaesia*, and *The Secret History of Hobgoblins*. His work has been published in *Spectrum Illustration Annuals* for science fiction and fantasy art, and he won a Silver Award in *Spectrum Annual* 15. Larry has always been interested in mythology, faerie tales, and folk tales, so turning to Inuit mythology was a natural step for him. He especially enjoys illustrating Inuit myths as they have rarely been illustrated previously.